3

First American Edition 2003
by Kane/Miller Book Publishers, Inc.
La Jolla, California

Original title in French, Figaro, le chat qui ronfle
By Jean-Baptiste Baronian and Martina Kinder
Production and copyright © Rainbow Grafics Intl – Baronian Books
English text © Rainbow Grafics Intl – Baronian Books

American English adaptation of this edition © Kane/Miller Book Publishers, Inc.
All rights reserved. For more information contact:
Kane/Miller Book Publishers
P.O. Box 8515
La Jolla, CA 92038
www.kanemiller.com

Library of Congress Control Number: 2003101411

1 2 3 4 5 6 7 8 9 10

ISBN 1-929132-53-0

To Pol

Figaro
The Cat Who Snored

Jean-Baptiste Baronian

Martina Kinder

Kane/Miller
BOOK PUBLISHERS

Everyday after lunch, Figaro had a little nap in the corner of the stable.

He'd close his eyes, start purring, and after just a few seconds he'd be fast asleep and snoring very, very loudly, just like a train.

Figaro snored so loud that everyone on the farm could hear him.

"When I bark," said the dog,
"it's to warn of danger.

What is Figaro's snoring for?"

"When I crow," said the rooster, "it's to wake the farm. What is Figaro's snoring for?"

"When I bray," said the donkey, "it's to welcome a visitor. What is Figaro's snoring for?"

The rooster, the dog and the donkey decided to talk to Figaro about his snoring. It really was unbearable.

"Who? Me?" exclaimed Figaro.
"You must be joking. I don't snore!"

"It's not just ordinary snoring. It's whirring, like an engine," said the rooster.

"Like a tractor engine!" added the donkey.

"It's just too loud," said the dog.

"What about having your nap away from the farm?" inquired the rooster.

"How about in the empty barn near the big oak tree?" suggested the dog.

"Are you asking me to leave?" sighed Figaro.

"No, no, not at all,"
said the donkey, hurriedly.

"It's just for your nap," agreed the rooster.

Figaro thought for a moment.
"Well, why not?" he said.
"As long as I'm left in peace, I can sleep anywhere."

Several days went by, then
one week, then another.

Figaro got used to having
his nap in the empty barn.
In fact, he spent more and
more time there. It was
such a peaceful, restful place
that he hardly went to the
farm at all anymore.

Then, one afternoon, just after he woke up, he heard strange noises outside the barn.

He peeked outside and saw his three old friends, the rooster, the donkey and the dog.

They looked very embarrassed.

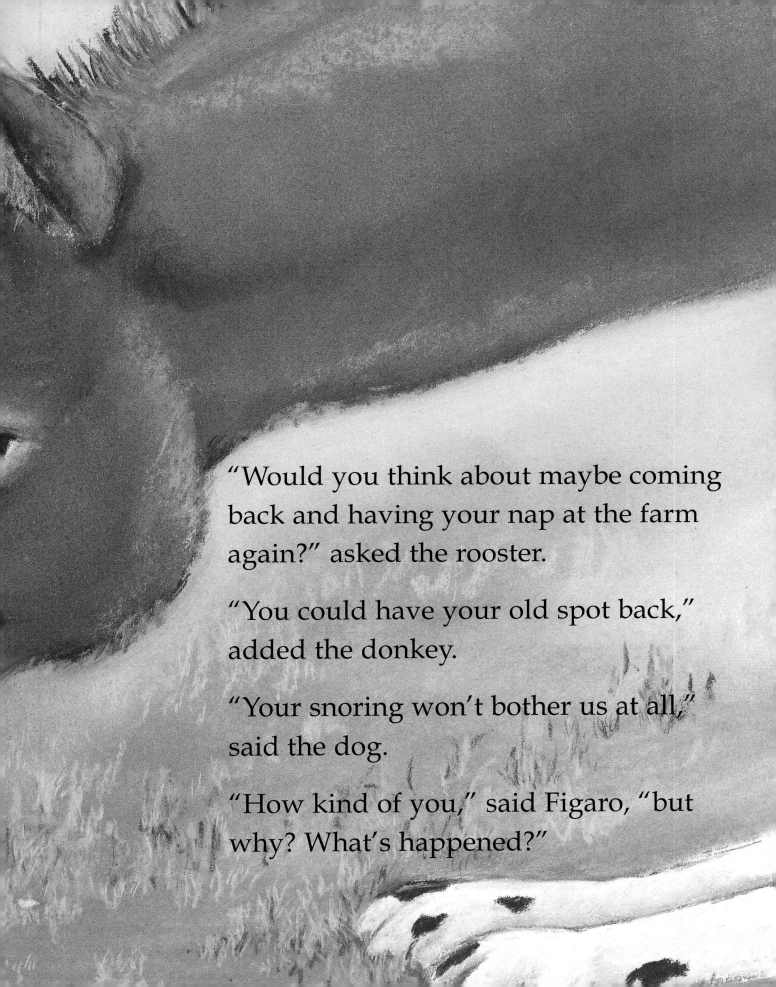

"Would you think about maybe coming back and having your nap at the farm again?" asked the rooster.

"You could have your old spot back," added the donkey.

"Your snoring won't bother us at all," said the dog.

"How kind of you," said Figaro, "but why? What's happened?"

"We miss you," said the rooster.

"And we need you," added the donkey.

"Since you've left the farm, there are mice everywhere!" the dog said. "Please come back, come back at once!"

Figaro's return was very noisy. The donkey brayed, the dog barked, and the rooster crowed.

And Figaro? Well, he purred very, very quietly.